THE 909

A FILM BY
MARK GIVENS
AND
JOEL HUSCHLE

BAMBOO
DART
PRESS

LOS ANGELES † NEW YORK † LONDON † MELBOURNE

The 909 by Mark Givens and Joel Huschle

ISBN: 978-1-947240-28-5

eISBN: 978-1-947240-29-2

First Printing 2021

Thanks to Tim Kirk for his technical expertise.

For information:

Bamboo Dart Press

chapbooks@bamboodartpress.com

Curated and operated by Dennis Callaci and Mark Givens

Bamboo Dart Press 014

www.pelekinesis.com   www.bamboodartpress.com   www.shrimperrecords.com

The 909 is a sci-fi script for a movie set in the near-future and taking the form of a reality documentary. The plot centers on a group of people who discuss the implications of "The Mesh", the technology that replaced the 'Net. Conspiracies, intrigue, and good old-fashioned camaraderie occupy these characters' thoughts as they try to retain a sense of individuality in an increasingly watchful society.

CAST

JOEL
A young man

AMY
A young woman

TIM
A friend

DIRECTOR
Off-screen voice

FIRST COUPLE
Two men drinking coffee

SECOND COUPLE
Two women sitting on a bench

VARIOUS INDIVIDUALS
milling about with cell phones

PARK WORKER
sweeping up feathers

LOCATIONS

VICTORIA GARDENS

An outdoor shopping mall in Rancho Cucamonga designed to look like an old public downtown, complete with artificial history and piped-in music, but still a privately-owned space.

ABANDONED STRIP MALLS

Strip malls along Foothill Blvd and Arrow Hwy, usually with gravel parking lots.

A CAR

Interior shots only.

BEST BUY, APPLE STORE, STARBUCKS

Exterior shots only.

THE
909

EXT. PARKING LOT - DAY

CLOSE-UP on Joel's feet walking on asphalt, kicking up dust.

The sound of crunching gravel.

> **DIRECTOR (VO)**
> Do you see Randy anymore?

> **JOEL**
> Distant Randy? No, I haven't seen him since, what... 2004?

Credit: "THE 909"

> **DIRECTOR (VO)**
> What's he been up to?

> **JOEL**
> I don't know. He's not in the 909 anymore.

We see Joel's feet walking across the asphalt, past some feathers.

Credit: "a film by Mark Givens and Joel Huschle"

CLOSE UP of Joel's profile. He is holding a Russian Nesting Penguin and he's cleaning it. He continues to walk.

JOEL
(to Director, questioningly)

What was that?

(CROSSTALK)

DIRECTOR (VO)
(muffled)

Where is he?

JOEL

Where is he? I don't know... Corona, maybe? Nowhere, everywhere... somewhere in the Mesh...

Music intro comes up, camera pulls back.

JOEL

Does it matter?

INT. CAR - DAY

Driving, camera is inside car, looking out the window as strip malls in various states of disrepair fly by.

Music kicks in.

> JOEL
>
> I think that was part of the point, really. Nobody really cares WHERE anybody is; location is just not important.

Music plays as the camera continues to drive by mini-malls in disrepair.

> JOEL (VO)
>
> It was different before The Overlay.

FADE OUT

INT. CAR - DAY

Joel in one car, pulls up next to a friend, Amy (in another car) and leans out the window.

Cars travel in straight lines (no turning).

> **AMY**
> Hey, how's it going?

> **JOEL**
> Pretty good. What are you up to?

> **AMY**
> Nothing much. Where you headed?

> **JOEL**
> Out to Walnut. Wanna grab a cup?

> **AMY**
> Sure! I'm going that way, too. Should we meet in, like, Diamond Bar?

                    JOEL
Sure. Where about?

                    AMY
I don't know. Downtown?

                    JOEL
There's not really a
'downtown' area of Diamond
Bar. Wanna just meet at the
Starbucks in the Apple store?

                    AMY
Which one?

                    JOEL
The one in the Best Buy?

                    AMY
Okay, see you there.

                              DISSOLVE TO:

EXT. COFFEE SHOP - DAY

Joel and Amy sit in the coffee
shop, a Starbucks inside the Apple

store inside the Best Buy, talking.

Camera outside, shooting in through the window. No audio from location, just incidental noise (coffee shop background noise, cups clanking...) No groups or couples, only solo patrons.

                    JOEL (VO)
     Sure, I was a little upset
     about The Overlay at first.
     But, I mean, they'd been
     working on it for a while.

Montage begins showing charts and graphs and cells dividing and people standing in groups.

                  DIRECTOR (VO)
     That was Blackpointe's thing,
     right?

                    JOEL (VO)
     No, this was before
     Blackpointe, back when we had
     numbers assigned to different
     areas.
          (continued)

JOEL (VO) CONT'D

We used to live in an area that, a long time ago, was coded "213", right? Then they broke that into two smaller parts and called them "213" and "714". Then they split up 714 into a couple parts and they kept splitting and dividing and regrouping.

CUT TO:

EXT. ART SHOT - DAY

CLOSE UP of Joel's face against an out-of-focus background.

JOEL

By the 1990s, with more people and faster computers, we started assigning codes ON TOP of these other codes. We started creating subgroups within subgroups, started using networks to keep track of things, started assigning
(continued)

JOEL CONT'D

codes to smaller and smaller
groups. Which made sense, I
guess.

I suppose if you have the
computing power and big enough
databases you can keep track
of all that. I guess that's
part of the point, too.

DISSOLVE TO:

EXT. ART SHOT - DAY

Feathers falling in front of the
Russian Nesting Penguin.

JOEL

I just didn't see a reason
to eliminate whatever groups
were already established, but
whatever.

CUT TO:

EXT. COFFEE SHOP - DAY

Joel and Amy in the window at coffee shop.

JOEL (VO)

You can break down a group into smaller and smaller subgroups until you just have one person in each group. That's a small group. Actually, that's not a group at all, that's just a person.

Through the window we see Joel and Amy exchange phones.

DIRECTOR (VO)

(laughs)

Yeah, that's just a point... or a... what?...

JOEL (VO)

Or just a node, yeah. A group of one.

Joel gets up and leaves. Amy takes another sip of coffee.

DISSOLVE TO:

Feathers falling in front of a coffee
cup in the dirt.

FADE OUT

EXT. PARK - DAY

If there are people in the shot
they are solo, not grouped. A park
worker is sweeping up feathers.

We see Joel walking through the park,
holding the Russian Nesting Penguin.
Slow motion close ups of people
as Joel passes them. Some exchange
phones. Some feathers fall.

> **JOEL (VO)**
> It was funny at first. People
> would joke about being their
> own area code. I guess we all
> are now.

> **DIRECTOR (VO)**
> But it makes sense now,
> doesn't it?

JOEL (VO)

Yeah, in retrospect it all makes sense. The Overlay replaced codes based on physical space with codes for individual people, numbers that could move from one place to another.

The old area codes were pretty meaningless by that point anyway. I remember people would call me and I'd be in Fontana and the number would be, like, 207 and I'd think '207? Isn't that Maine?' And it's actually my friend, Distant Randy, and he's just down at the 7-Eleven on Summit. So it didn't really make any difference in that sense.

CUT TO:

Joel sitting on a picnic table.

JOEL

What I don't think anyone thought about was what it would do to the groups of people in the area, people we're friends with in person. I mean, we all have our friends and our groups in the Mesh but are we sacrificing personal relationships by swapping out one artificially created "family" for another? And what about our local groups?

DIRECTOR (VO)

What do you mean? Like, face-to-face?

JOEL

Yeah, people we meet for coffee.

DIRECTOR (VO)

Like Amy?

JOEL

Yeah, like Amy.

DIRECTOR (VO)

How long have you known her?

JOEL

We've been friends for a
while. Amy is still in the
909.

Joel's phone rings.

JOEL

Hello? Oh, hey Tim.

    (pause)

Yeah, sure.

    (responding to the question
    "Where do you want to meet?")

What about downtown?

    (responding to the suggestion
    "how about Victoria
    Gardens?")

Victoria Gardens!? That's not
a downtown, it's a mall.

    (responding to "it looks
    like a downtown")

I know, but it's a mall.

    (continued)

JOEL CONT'D
(responding to "I know, but I
still want to meet there.")

Yeah, okay. I'll meet you
there.

(to the Director, off screen)

We're meeting "downtown" at
Victoria Gardens.

(laughs)

FADE OUT

EXT. CAR - DAY

Joel is driving past decaying mini-
malls. Camera is in the passenger
seat, looking at Joel. Car travels in
a straight line.

DIRECTOR (VO)
So how did The Overlay
lay the groundwork for the
Mesh? Wasn't that really the
catalyst that...

JOEL

Without The Overlay, we'd
still be using the internet,
yeah. But once The Overlay
was in place and everyone had
a number, it became easier
to map data between points.
We finally got away from the
idea that data had to travel
through some central hub,
across some common lines.

CUT TO:

feathers falling on a bicycle rim
(metaphorically, spoke and hub)

JOEL

Each person became a unique
location for sending and
receiving data to any other
point. And that's how the Mesh
was born.

DIRECTOR (VO)

That's what Blackpointe
invented, right? After he
split with the military?

                    JOEL
     Yeah, but it's based on stuff
     Bram Cohen did at the turn of
     the century.

                              DISSOLVE TO:

backlit cheesecloth.

                  JOEL (VO)
     And now everyone is a node
     - a transmitter as well as
     a receiver so it's almost
     impossible for a government to
     take the Mesh down. Or anyone.
     Take out a node and the data
     will just find another route
     to get to where it needs to
     go.

                                  CUT TO:

INT. CAR - DAY

Joel driving past decaying mini-
malls.

                    JOEL

It's kind of funny to me that
Col. Blackpointe worked so
hard to develop something
that the government could not
control. But I'm glad he did!

                    DISSOLVE TO:

EXT. STREET - DAY

*Camera in car, shooting out the
window while driving past decaying
mini-malls.*

                JOEL (VO)

Of course, there have always
been people who didn't like
the idea.

                DIRECTOR (VO)

There always are.

                JOEL (VO)

Yeah, that's true.

CUT TO:

INT. CAR - DAY

                    JOEL
    I know what they're talking
    about and it's what we're
    fighting for, too. For the
    Mesh to work, everyone needs
    to stay connected to the Mesh.
    It runs faster when more
    people are using it. We all
    know that. But that also means
    that the government knows
    exactly where everyone is at
    all times.

Joel turns into a parking lot. (this
is a turning point.)

                    FADE OUT

EXT. VICTORIA GARDENS - DAY

A couple is sitting at a table. In the
background, a few people exchange

phones. No one is talking to each other.

The couple at a table is using mobile devices.

MAN 1

Sure, we were a little nervous about having "Big Brother" watching us all the time. Cameras and that sort of thing; that's really intrusive. But you can't even SEE the little Mesh nodes – you almost don't even know they're there!

MAN 2

Except that you're connected wherever...

MAN 1

Yeah. So it's totally worth it.

JOEL (VO)

(points to mobile device)

Don't you worry about the one that's ON you?

                    MAN 1
          (puzzled)
     Well, how else would you get
     on the mesh?

                                        CUT TO:

Some feathers drift down.

                                        CUT TO:

A different couple sitting on a
bench, watching children.

                    WOMAN 1
     I don't understand what you
     mean.

                    WOMAN 2
     He's talking about those
     "Privacy Concerns" that people
     used to talk about. Remember
     that guy Andy?

                    WOMAN 1
     Randy?

WOMAN 2

Yeah, Randy. Remember how he used to go on about how the government was watching him?

WOMAN 1

That sounds familiar.

WOMAN 2

(to Woman 1)

Look him up.

Woman 1 types on her mobile device.

Anyway, I don't think it's that big of a deal. I mean, we still have privacy.

WOMAN 1

(pointing at a picture of Randy on her device)

Oh, yeah! I remember that guy. He was pretty nuts.

WOMAN 2

See? I told you.

(looks around)

He's not here, is he?

WOMAN 1

No, no. He's in..

(looking at the screen)

uh... Norco right now.

Camera follows Joel as he walks away.

JOEL

So the Mesh can be pretty useful, obviously, and people don't even think about it. The "Mesh Nodes" that he was talking about are these little stationary nodes they put up to reinforce the system. They're not as strong as the one's people carry

(points to cellphone)

but they help. And they make it possible for us to do what we need to do out here.

Joel approaches the table where Tim is sitting. Some magazines are on the table.

JOEL

Hey, Tim.

                        TIM
        Hey, Joel.

They exchange phones. In the
background, a cop is taking away a
person in handcuffs.

                        TIM
        What's up? Anyone else around
        today?

                        JOEL
        Yeah, I ran into Amy. She's
        doing all right. You?

                        TIM
No. No one.

                        JOEL
            (reaching for a magazine)
        Oh, Is that ME?

The magazine is called "Me Magazine"
and there is a picture of Joel on the
cover. Joel picks it up and starts
flipping through it.

                    TIM
I lost touch with 15 people
last week. They didn't show
up.

                    JOEL
That's a drag.

                    TIM
Yeah. That's the way it goes.

Joel and Tim sit for a moment. A
feather falls on the table.

Music come up.

                                    CUT TO:

EXT. ART SEQUENCE - DAY

CLOSE-UP of a badminton birdie.
Camera follows it flying through the
air.

                    JOEL (VO)
I'm concerned about the
privacy stuff, sure. The
            (continued)

JOEL (VO) CONT'D

Overlay just seemed like
a really dangerous way to
accomplish something that
probably would have happened
anyway. I was worried about
most of the SocialWeb privacy
stuff, too, and we all know
how that turned out. The Mesh
is no different.

The birdie lands in a box, kicking up
some feathers.

DISSOLVE TO:

EXT. STREET - DAY

*Camera in car, shooting out the
window while driving past decaying
mini-malls.*

JOEL (VO)

The privacy issues are just
some of the things we're
fighting. I don't want to go

(continued)

JOEL (VO) CONT'D

through life worrying about
whether I'm doing something
that I might get in trouble
for, you know? And I can't
believe this has been going on
for so long now. I think we've
lost touch in a way. When
everything goes global, what
happens to the local?

CUT TO:

EXT. FIELD - DUSK

long shot of Joel at dusk,
silhouetted, walking across a dirt
field.

JOEL (VO)

I don't know. We still have a
lot of work to do. But we can
do it.

CUT TO:

EXT. FIELD - DUSK

Joel's feet walking through piles
of feathers.

> ### JOEL (VO)
> I mean, I still think it's
> important to build networks
> of people, not data. We
> started with nine hundred
> and nine people, giving us
> a name and a purpose. We're
> down a few right now, but
> we're not going to give up.
> Not for anything.

Something shiny moves in front of
the camera. Joel stops talking and
follows it off-screen.

FADE OUT

THE TECHNOLOGY IN THE BOOK, A DECADE OUT, IS OBVIOUSLY CLOSER TO A REALITY NOW THAN IT WAS WHEN WRITTEN.

The advances in mesh networking serve as the impetus for getting this story out there into the world now, before the speculation becomes retrospeculative. Regardless of the actual technology, the conceptual underpinnings are strong.

Technology sets the stage for the actions of *The 909* and from this technological base, *The 909* explores surveillance, place, and autonomy. It's also about the way we group people and keep track of them with programs

like ZIP codes and addresses.
For example, one component of
The 909 is based on the overlay
plan, a program started in 1992
that dislocated, or de-located,
groups from their associated
areas by overlaying one area
code on top of another.

 In *The 909*, we speculate
that eventually each person
will have their own number,
becoming a singular data point,
a group of one. This idea fits
perfectly with the idea of the
mesh; each point in the mesh
is a transmitter as well as a
receiver, the overlay assigns
numbers to those points.
So, *The 909* questions the
ramifications of this kind of
interconnectedness.

**THE BOOK PLAYS WITH THE OPEN
SPACES OF THE INLAND EMPIRE,
THE FORMER VINEYARD THAT IS
NOW A GROSS OUTDOOR MALL CALLED
VICTORIA GARDENS, VACANT STRIP**

MALLS, CORPORATE COFFEE SHOPS HOUSED IN A HUGE CHAIN STORE, A STRETCH OF ROAD IN NORCO, THESE SPACES BECOME INCREDIBLY IMPORTANT IN TYING INTO THE THEME OF THE TECHNOLOGY OF THE "MESH," SOMETHING THAT IS A CONSTANT ABSTRACTION COMPANION MARRIED TO THE PHYSICALITY OF THE IE.

The idea of systems without centers, without a central point, is intriguing. Instead of a spoke-and-hub model, these systems resemble other peer-to-peer systems; de-centralized systems that eliminate the biggest choke point and allowing data to route around any blockages that may occur. Information will find a way through. This is true for data systems as well as physical spaces.

Diamond Bar, for example, is a town built without a fixed center while Victoria Gardens

is a shopping mall masquerading
as a downtown — one model
denying place, the other trying
desperately to create one. So
this is really an exploration
of the delocation of public
spaces, the absence of place,
of belonging. In one way it's
demoralizing, but there's
something tragically beautiful
about places that nobody wants.
Something communal, a shared
absence.

112 N. Harvard Ave. #65
Claremont, CA 91711

chapbooks@bamboodartpress.com
www.bamboodartpress.com

www.ingramcontent.com/pod-product-compliance
Lightning Source LLC
Chambersburg PA
CBHW080756120626
46557CB00006B/1294